THE HOLOCAUST
A Young Boy's Story

SURVIVORS

THE HOLOCAUST
A Young Boy's Story

Stewart Ross

(adapted from an original manuscript by Andor Guttmann)

WAYLAND

Text copyright © 2001 Stewart Ross
Volume copyright © 2001 Wayland

Book editor: Katie Orchard
Map illustrator: Peter Bull

This edition published in 2015 by Wayland

Dewey number: 823.9'14 [J]
ISBN: 978 0 7502 9642 7

10 9 8 7 6 5 4 3 2 1

Wayland
An imprint of
Hachette Children's Group
Part of Hodder & Stoughton
Carmelite House
50 Victoria Embankment
London EC4Y 0DZ

An Hachette UK company
www.hachette.co.uk
www.hachettechildrens.co.uk

Printed and bound in Great Britain by
Clays Ltd, St Ives plc

Introduction

The Holocaust: A Young Boy's Story is based on the remarkable true story of Andor ('Bandi') Guttmann, a Hungarian Jew who lived in Budapest during the Second World War. It begins in the spring of 1944.

During the 1930s, Hungary had been on good terms with Nazi Germany. When Germany attacked Russia in 1941, Hungary and Germany became allies. By the spring of 1944, the Germans were in retreat. Russian troops overran Romania and advanced into Hungary. The airforces of Britain and the USA, Russia's allies, started bombing Budapest and other Hungarian cities. Hungary's pro-fascist government began to waver.

In March 1944, the Germans learned that the Hungarians were thinking of making peace. They responded by sending their own troops into Hungary. As the fighting grew more fierce, the Germans tightened their control over the country. The SS, which had already massacred millions of Jews elsewhere in Europe, stepped up its campaign against

Hungary's Jews. Hungarian fascists, the Arrow Cross, eagerly joined in the persecution. For the thousands of Jews living in Budapest, life became a nightmare.

This map shows Hungary in 1944, the period in which this story takes place.

This book is dedicated to victims of racism everywhere and in every age.

One

A Target

'What a stupid time to bring in a new law!' complained Mother crossly. She looked up from sewing the yellow star on to my school pullover. 'It's a waste of time with only one day to go.'

It was early morning on 16 April, the last day of the school year. The Hungarian government had said that from now on all Jews had to wear a Star of David on the outside of their clothes.

I shrugged my shoulders. 'Probably someone's weird sense of humour,' I suggested.

Mother laughed. I smiled at the sound, which reminded me of happier days.

'What sense of humour, Bandi?' she asked. 'More likely some idiot didn't check his diary. Typical of the fools that run the country nowadays.' She bent over her sewing again and I went to my room to get my school-books.

The law made us a marked people, set aside by a badge of race. It was supposed to shame us, but it didn't. OK, I was angry because the star would make life more difficult, but it

1

also made me proud. It proved I was something special. A Jew. I had never wanted to be anything else and nothing during the unspeakable horrors that followed made me change my mind.

A few hours later, I, Bandi Guttmann, was sitting on the school bench on the last day of term with my Star of David glowing on the front of my pullover. Mother had stitched it on just above the heart, like a target. Luckily, hardly anyone aimed at it. At least, not then.

Only a few Jews were allowed in our smart, all boys' secondary school. The only other Jew in our class had dropped out a few weeks before. As I was the only boy with a star, for the moment I was the centre of attention. Some boys were spiteful. Most just gave me odd looks, as if I had gone home the previous day as one person and returned the next day as someone different.

A few of the younger boys were fascinated, almost jealous. One actually called me 'sheriff' because my star reminded him of the badge lawmen wore in cowboy films. For the rest of the day I was his leader. It was not exactly what the Nazis had intended when they ordered us to wear the Star of David.

My classmates were in high spirits because, thanks to the war, school was ending early. Five months of holiday stretched ahead of them. They knew it wouldn't be like holidays before the war, but like most teenage boys they didn't think too carefully about such things.

For the teachers it was different. Most of them were unsure what to do. Now I was marked as a Jew, should they ignore me or bully me? If they treated me as before, they might be reported to the authorities as pro-Jewish. They got round it by ignoring me. If they spoke to me, they looked elsewhere, trying not to catch my eye. I realize now they were not just afraid. They were ashamed.

That afternoon I was threatened by a gang of boys waiting for Jews outside the school gates. They shoved me up against a wall and said they were going to beat me up. They called me 'Hebrew scum' and 'money-grabber', expressions they had picked up from the radio and other Nazi propaganda. Their eyes were wild with the unthinking cruelty of the pack, like wolves.

I couldn't fight my way out, so I kept quiet and waited to see what would happen next. For some reason, no one wanted to be the first to hit me. Then someone said, 'It's not his fault he's a Jew, is it?' That set them arguing and in the end they let me go. It's strange, but children often see things to which adults are blind.

My mother was furious when I told her what had happened. She sent me straight to her sewing box to fetch her scissors.

Snipping away the stitching that held on my yellow star, she said defiantly, 'Right! That's simple. From now on we won't wear these silly badges. None of us!'

When she had finished, she exclaimed, 'There! Now

3

you're just an ordinary Hungarian like everyone else.'

If only it had been that simple.

Two

The Arrow Cross

It would have been pointless wearing the Star of David in our apartment block. Everyone knew we were Jews, just as we knew the family in the basement were gypsies and the German couple next door were Nazis. Until the Germans occupied our country, no one bothered much about such things. We were too busy trying to get by.

Father was very patriotic. He had fought in the First World War, been wounded and had medals to show for his bravery. At the start of the Second World War, aged forty-three, he was again called up into the army. Mother and I went to the barracks to say goodbye. The other soldiers whistled and tried to chat her up because she was still a very beautiful woman. I was there as a sort of sign that she was not available, I suppose.

I had two older sisters, Agi and Edith, and one younger, Katie. Once Father had gone, like other poor families in Budapest our life became a long, hard struggle. Mother and Agi found what work they could, although it was not easy.

Few Hungarians dared openly employ a Jew. For Mother this was particularly humiliating. She was a proud woman: proud of her family, proud of her faith and proud of her home, and she fought to maintain them with all her strength. It was her determination and intelligence that held us together, just as her quick thinking saved our lives on more than one occasion.

Budapest is a city of two parts, Buda and Pest. They are divided by the River Danube. We lived in Pest, in a working-class slum near the river. After dark, women hung about idly on street corners and gangs of yobs patrolled the alleys. Opposite us was a large building with a bar in the basement. This was where the Hungarian fascists, the Arrow Cross (we called them 'Arrowers'), met to drink and argue with the socialists and anyone else who opposed them. Arrowers were terrible people, just thugs who used fascism as an excuse to throw their weight around. They started fights almost every night but the police didn't dare do anything about them because the Arrow Cross had the support of the Germans.

Our building was typical of many in the district: a large, two-storey apartment block built around a dark courtyard. Its sagging gutters, small windows and peeling yellow paint gave it a depressing look of faded glory. When we were younger, what we liked most about the house were the iron railings of the balconies. We used to run round the court-yard clattering a stick against the railings – rat-tat-tat! – until

6

one of the neighbours came out to complain about the noise.

The part of the block we didn't like was the attic, a gloomy place of ghosts and cobwebs. We used to put out our washing to dry up there until a woman hanged herself from one of the rafters. After that, we didn't dare go into the attic again and dried our clothes in the kitchen instead.

By the time we had to wear the Star of David I was used to Jews being picked on. Although I was tall and strong, I had learned how to avoid trouble without getting into fist-fights. That's why I didn't resist when those boys threatened to beat me up after school. Mother had taught me that we had no chance if we tried to meet force with force. The only way to survive was to keep our mouths shut, our eyes open and never, ever, give up.

I first met anti-Jewish racism long before the war. We used to live in the north of Hungary, in a pretty village surrounded by hills and vineyards. All I can remember about it were the flowers that grew in the fields and gardens and danced in the painted wooden boxes that stood on every window-sill.

Father was the village baker. It was a good business and we owned a large house with its own orchard and spring of fresh water. Then a fascist baker moved in. He spread foul rumours about us and told the villagers that they should not buy Jewish bread. Father's business soon collapsed and we were forced to move to Budapest to find work.

The move turned out to be a blessing in disguise. During the war, the Arrow Cross rounded up all the Jews in the north and sent them abroad to death camps. I don't think any survived.

Three

Ruth

Katie looked up at the poster. *'Any person hiding, giving shelter to, or otherwise assisting a runaway Jew,'* she read, *'shall be executed. By order, the Government.'* She whistled softly through her teeth. 'Wow, Bandi!' she exclaimed. 'That means us.'

Without thinking, I kicked her on the shin. 'Shut up!' I hissed.

She gave a yelp of pain and turned to me with tears in her eyes. 'What was that for, Bandi? It really hurt.'

I felt bad. 'I'm sorry, Katie,' I said, putting my arm round her shoulders and leading her across the street towards our house. 'It's just that you never know who's listening. That bar, the one where the poster is, it's always full of Arrowers. If they heard you . . .'

I didn't need to finish the sentence. Katie wiped her eyes on her sleeve. 'Sorry, Bandi,' she sniffed. 'You were think-ing of Uncle Lionel and Ruth, weren't you?'

I nodded.

As we entered the dim hall of our apartment block, she

paused. 'You're quite fond of Ruth, aren't you, Bandi?'

I felt myself blushing. To hide my embarrassment, I ran towards the staircase. 'Come on, slowcoach!' I yelled. 'Race you to the top!'

Uncle Lionel and his daughter Ruth were on the run. They had escaped from northern Hungary, near where we had once lived, and made their way to Budapest. Finding our building, they had crept up to our flat late one night. They had been with us a week now, keeping clear of the windows and hardly daring to speak. If one of the Nazi supporters who lived in the block suspected we were sheltering Jewish refugees, the flat would be searched and – well, the poster made it clear what would happen.

Ruth was fourteen, the same age as me. She had wide, dark eyes and black hair tied back from her face with a ribbon. Because she could not go out, I stayed in and talked to her for hours. The more we talked, the more fond of her I became. Once we discussed the places we would like to visit together.

'What about Vienna?' I suggested. 'Or Paris? Or London? Maybe even New York!'

'Oh, Bandi,' she laughed, taking hold of my hand, 'what a dreamer you are! So when are we going to go to all these glamorous cities?'

'After the war,' I replied eagerly. 'When the Nazis have been defeated and Hungary is free again.'

She sighed and looked at me with those black, mournful

eyes. 'After the war, Bandi? And do you think we'll still be alive then?'

A shadow seemed to fall across the room. 'Of course we'll be alive,' I replied. I tried to laugh but the sound stuck in my throat.

That night Ruth and her father moved to another address. As I soon discovered for myself, staying one step ahead of the authorities was the only way to survive. A moving target is more difficult to hit than a stationary one. But I don't know whether it worked for Ruth and Uncle Lionel. I suspect it didn't because we never saw or heard from them again.

We saw very little of Father now. Sometimes he turned up on leave, emerging like a figure out of the mist, then vanishing again a day or two later. One night when he was at home a group of Arrowers from the bar opposite got roaring drunk and staggered across the road towards our apartment block. 'We're coming to get you, Jewish scum!' they roared, scrabbling in the dirt for stones to throw at our windows.

Father ordered us all into a back room and opened the door that led on to the balcony. 'Yes?' he called, stepping forward so they could see him. 'What do you want?'

There were a few more shouts, then silence. Father came back into the room and locked the door. He was wearing his uniform. In one hand he carried a stout stick, in the other his army revolver.

'Snivelling cowards!' he snorted.

I hoped he would still be at home the next time Arrowers decided to pay us a visit.

Four

The Pilot

A few days later I was sitting in the flat on my own, listening to the radio. The rest of the family was out. Mother and Agi were working. Edith and Katie were visiting friends.

Suddenly, the Hungarian broadcast was interrupted by an urgent voice: '*Achtung! Achtung! Lichtspiele!*' It was an air-raid warning. For some reason – perhaps to give the Germans more time to take shelter – the warnings were now given first in German then repeated in Hungarian. I stayed where I was, waiting to hear the name of the target.

'*Achtung!* Budapest!' Without bothering to turn off the radio, I ran out of the flat, down the stairs and into the cellar. I was the first to arrive. The war had taught me to be wary, to check every building, every room I entered to see where the safest place was. From my previous visits I knew that the safest point of the cellar was the corner furthest from the door. I hurried over there and hid myself away in the shadows.

The rest of the people in the apartment block hurried in over the next five minutes. The gypsies huddled together along one wall. The Nazi couple sat grim faced and upright on a wooden bench. The rest, some bringing blankets and parcels of food, arranged themselves around the cellar as best they could.

It was then that I noticed the stranger, a mournful-looking young man in the uniform of an airforce pilot. He soon became the centre of attention, bombarded with questions from all sides. 'Yes,' he replied, he was back from the Eastern Front.

'What was it like?'

He gave a forlorn smile. 'Like hell, except colder.' He had bombed Russian villages, of course, '. . . but when you're flying high you don't see much. Just little dots of houses. It's difficult to imagine the people in them . . .'

The cross-examination was interrupted by a low drone. Bombers! Someone put out the oil-lamp and we waited in the dark for the raid to begin.

The noise of the approaching planes grew louder. Then came the rapid *Boom! Boom!* of anti-aircraft fire. Seconds later, the bombs began to fall. A chilling whistle, a pause, then the heavy thump of explosion. On and on it went, bomb after bomb. The walls of the cellar shivered. Clouds of choking dust fell from the ceiling. A woman lying next to me was praying wildly, 'Oh, merciful God, don't let it hit me! Please don't let it hit me!'

I closed my eyes and put my hands over my ears to block out the noise. I thought of my mother, hoping she was safe. I imagined her face, young and smiling on one of our

Sunday afternoon picnics on the banks of the river. I saw her walking in her best clothes, graceful, proud. Who was she meeting? That man with the film-star looks? It definitely wasn't Father . . . I tried not to think any more. The past had its sadness, too.

At last the bombing stopped. The lamp was lit and we looked around, dazed and frightened.

The Nazi woman noticed me for the first time. 'Well, Jew-boy,' she asked in a loud voice, 'I suppose you're pleased that the British pigs are bombing us?'

I didn't reply but one of the gypsies said, 'Leave him alone.'

The woman snorted.

Then the pilot looked across at me. His face was very pale. He said quietly, 'If we got a direct hit, he'd be killed the same as us.' With that, he stood up and left the cellar. I followed after him as quickly as I could but when I got outside he had disappeared. I had not even thanked him.

Luckily, our apartment block had not been damaged. Even the glass in the windows was unbroken. Several bombs had fallen further down the street, near the hospital. I locked the door of the flat and went out to have a look.

Where tall houses had stood only an hour before there were now just piles of smoking rubble. Firemen, policemen, soldiers and civilian volunteers were sifting through the broken bricks and timber, looking for survivors.

Smoke and dust hung in the hot summer air. There was a strange stench, too, one I had never smelled before. Sweet, like a very rich honey. Watching a rescue party carrying away a charred body on a stretcher, I suddenly realized what it was. The smell of burned flesh.

I shuddered and turned for home.

Five

Humiliation

In May, a couple of months after my fourteenth birthday, I met our elderly postman puffing up the stairs with an important-looking letter.

'Who's it for?' I asked.

'You, Bandi,' he replied. 'And I reckon I know what it is, too. Bad luck, lad!'

My heart sank. I also knew what the letter contained. At the age of fourteen, all boys had to do military service to prepare them for the army. Inside the official brown envelope were my call-up papers.

As in everything else, Jews were kept separate for military training. Hungarians were taught rifle drill, map-reading and other military skills. Friends who had been on the course told me it was hard work but quite exciting. The training offered to Jewish recruits was rather different.

On the appointed day I made my way to the parade ground where the Jewish group had been told to meet. It was a dingy place, a sort of sunken garden with a wall on one side

17

and trees and broken-down huts on the other. I reckon it had been chosen because it was hidden from view. Our officers didn't want anyone snooping on what happened.

There were about thirty recruits, some of whom I already knew. Josh had been at primary school with me, and I had met Peter and Sam at the synagogue before it was closed down. Peter, a tall, very pale boy, came from an orthodox Jewish family who took their religion very seriously. He had his hair cut in the special orthodox way, with long side locks.

For about ten minutes we all milled about in the middle of the parade ground, looking anxiously across at the three officers who stood with their backs to us chatting under the trees.

Suddenly, they swung round and came marching towards us. The leader, a red-faced man of about forty-five, began shouting a torrent of abuse. 'Good God!' he bellowed. 'You snivelling Jewish rats! How dare you slop around like that! You can't get up to your cranky, depraved customs here. Get in your ranks this instant, or I'll make you regret you were ever born! Filthy dregs!'

Terrified, we lined up in three ranks.

The commander continued his abuse while the other officers walked between us, kicking and punching at random. Josh was hit across the face with a staff, making his nose bleed heavily. Not daring to move, he stood there as the blood trickled down his chin and over the front of his white shirt. Luckily, I escaped punishment.

★ ★ ★

The next four hours were a nightmare, the first time I had met anti-Jewish hatred face to face. We began with an hour's marching, up and down in the hot sun. And always the same senseless abuse, kicks and blows.

After the marching came the lecture. For two hours our commander explained why we, the Jews, were the lowest scum on Earth. Most of the time he screamed at us. Occasionally, like a bad actor, he smiled and, in a voice that fell almost to a whisper, told us how lucky we were to be in his kind, caring hands.

How I hated him!

When the lecture was over, the commander strolled slowly towards us. Reaching Peter, he stopped and grabbed him by the side lock. 'What the hell's this?' he demanded.

Peter turned pale. 'It's my side lock, sir,' he stammered. 'We have to wear—'

'Have to wear?' screamed the bully. '*Have to?*' The only thing you *have to* do, Jewish filth, is what I say. And I say I won't have any girly-haired sissy in my squad.'

Taking a pair of scissors from his pocket, he cut off Peter's side locks and waved them in the air. 'The same goes for the lot of you,' he yelled. 'Right! Kneel down for an honest Hungarian army trim.'

Half an hour's careless hacking left us all with bleeding scalps and disfigured hair. The humiliation was complete.

Dismissing us, the commander told us to return the next day wearing work clothes and carrying a shovel.

'Fat chance!' I muttered to myself. 'You won't see me again, whatever the consequences.'

Six

Star Houses

I worried all the way home. I didn't care about my messy hair. People stared at me, but I was used to that since we had started wearing the Star of David again. We had to or our Nazi neighbours would have called in the Arrow Cross. No, what really worried me was what I was going to do.

I couldn't go back to those bullies. I knew what would happen. We'd be set to work in the city, then moved somewhere else, and when we were too exhausted to work any more . . . It wasn't worth thinking about. So I wasn't going back. Which meant they'd come looking for me. Tomorrow morning? In a week? A month?

When Mother and my sisters saw the scissor cuts on my head and I told them what had happened, they agreed I had to stay away.

After we had talked for a bit, my little sister asked the question that was on everyone's mind. 'But, Bandi, if you don't do what the government orders, then you're a sort of runaway, aren't you?'

'I suppose so, Katie,' I nodded.

'Then if you're a runaway and we look after you, it's like Uncle Lionel and Ruth. I mean, the punishment is what we read on the poster.' She ran over to Mother and threw her arms round her neck. 'Oh, Mummy,' she sobbed, 'why has everything gone so horrible?'

I hardly slept a wink that night. I kept waking up and listening for the sound of marching feet. I was sure the commander had seen the look on my face and sent soldiers to force me to join the work party. To my great relief, no one came.

At dawn, I went and sat by the window to watch the street below. Morning slipped into afternoon and still no one came. In the evening the usual gang of Arrowers gathered in the bar opposite. Not once did they even glance up at our windows.

When I finally fell asleep, a tiny seed of hope had planted itself in my heart. Maybe the commander of the Jewish group had enough workers and couldn't be bothered to go looking for a straggler? Whatever the reason, we were still safe.

I watched the street for a week. The only visitor was Mrs Rabin, a family friend whose son was in the army. She brought bad news. All Jewish soldiers had been dismissed and made to join Workers' Brigades. These were bands of slaves, forced to do whatever the army wanted. She had heard that Father was in one of these brigades.

I thought about Father a lot then. He was so proud of his record as a soldier, of his medals and other mementoes. How stupid it was to take a dedicated man like that out of the front line! I felt so sorry for him. His problems with Mother before the war – their arguments and love affairs – didn't seem important any more. All that mattered was that he stayed alive.

In the end, it wasn't the soldiers who came. It was the police. I saw them working their way down the street, knocking on doors and checking names on clipboards. I was sure they were looking for me. Terrified, I ran up to the attic and hid myself under some old pieces of carpet. From my hiding place I could see the beam from which the woman had hanged herself. The frayed end of the rope was still there. Do they hang runaways, I wondered?

I heard heavy footsteps on the main staircase and a knock on a door. I couldn't tell which one. Voices, male and female, then footsteps going back down the stairs. They'd gone!

A few minutes later, Edith called up to me. 'Bandi! You can come down now.' Her voice sounded odd somehow.

Mother and the girls were standing together in the kitchen. The younger two were sobbing. Agi, her arm round Mother's waist, was shaking violently.

'What's the matter?' I asked. 'They didn't want me, did they?'

'No, Bandi,' said Mother slowly. 'They didn't want you.

23

They wanted all of us. Every Jew in Budapest is being moved into what they call Star Houses.'

Seven

The Move

I was horrified. 'Why?' I asked. 'They know where we are. Why do they want to move us to Star Houses?'

Mother shook her head. 'Don't look for logic, Bandi. It disappeared the moment Hitler came to power. The government wants all Jews to live together so it knows where to find them. Then there will be more room for Hungarians.'

'But we *are* Hungarians—'

'What did I say, Bandi?' interrupted Mother. 'No logic. No reason. Don't argue, and remember: keep your mouth shut, your eyes open and never, ever, give up. So let's get going. We have thirty-six hours to get out.'

We spent the rest of the day preparing for the move. Mother filled in the papers saying who we were, where we lived now and our new address. This, the police had told her, was a house on the Rakotzy-ut, a main street in a fashionable district of the city.

'The poorer we are,' she said with a smile as she put the

address on the form, 'the nicer our house. If we become beggars, perhaps they'll give us a palace.'

Edith, Katie and I did the packing. Agi went to ask some Hungarian friends if we could borrow their handcart. They were kindly people and an hour later Agi came clattering back up the street dragging the cart behind her. 'We're in luck,' she announced. 'Half the city seems to be packing up and there aren't nearly enough carts to go round. I was stopped several times on the way back and offered a fortune for mine.'

The next morning we loaded our possessions on to the cart. We couldn't take much, just a few clothes, cooking utensils, bedding and – Mother's orders – just one luxury each. I couldn't decide if I should take my stamp album. In the end I gave it to one of the gypsy boys and took the best of Father's war books instead. Katie cried bitterly when she had to leave all but one of her dolls behind. Mother, who loved beautiful things, took a Dresden china vase.

After we had said goodbye to our friends, the Nazi woman suddenly came hurrying out of the house. Looking about to check no one was watching, she grasped Mother by the hand. 'I'm so sorry,' she said. 'I know we haven't been friends and, to be honest, I don't like the Jews. But I never thought it would come to this. Good luck, Mrs Guttmann. I hope you will be all right.'

I think she meant what she said. Like most Germans, she had gone along with the crowd, not really thinking. Then, when the terrible truth dawned, it was too late to do anything about it. By ignoring the little sparks of racism, she and others like her had let them grow into a huge blaze they could not control.

As Agi had said, half the city seemed to be moving. The streets were crowded with handcarts, horse-drawn carts and poorer families struggling with suitcases and bundles humped on their shoulders. The refugees were largely women, children and the elderly. Most of the men, like Father, had been called up long ago.

A few children cried and Arrow Cross youths shouted abuse at us from time to time. But for the most part the only sound was shuffling feet and the rumble of cart wheels on the cobbles. I remember thinking of it as a kind of music, like the sad, slow march played at funerals.

As we passed, non-Jewish citizens stared at us from windows and doorsteps. One or two waved or gave us the thumbs-up sign for good luck. There were few smiles. Occasionally, a woman came out with a small gift of food or money. The ordinary people of Budapest didn't like what was happening any more than we did.

Mother was right – our house on Rakotzy-ut was very grand, better than anywhere we had lived before. As we rested outside before unloading our cart, Edith asked why we had been sent to such a mansion.

'Probably because they don't expect us to be here for long,' Mother replied.

'Really? Where are we going next?' Edith asked innocently.

Mother sighed. 'I don't know, Edith, dear. And I don't want to know. It's best not to ask.'

Eight

Body and Mind

Our new house was one of hundreds of 'Jews' Houses' scattered around the city. Their nickname – 'Star Houses' – was obvious: almost everyone who lived there had to wear the yellow Star of David.

Our flat, although small, was comfortable enough. Mother soon had it looking quite respectable, with the Dresden vase in pride of place on the mantelpiece. She was far too proud to let our standards slip just because we had been moved. Unfortunately, we had to share the flat with a grumpy, middle-aged woman who didn't get on with anyone. It's odd how some people refuse to co-operate, even when there is no point in trying to go it alone.

She wasn't our only problem. The building next door, which had once been a hotel, had been taken over by the Germans. It was now shared between the dreaded SS and officers of the regular German army. Luckily for us, there was little love lost between the two groups.

All Jews now had to obey a curfew. This meant we had to stay indoors, apart from a couple of hours in the afternoon when we were allowed out to go shopping for food. Not that there was much food to buy. A dish of potatoes was a feast and we were hungry all the time. Any Jew found breaking the curfew could be shot on sight.

Apart from the warden, there was one other non-Jew in our house. He was an old-fashioned cavalry general who had retired long ago. He was a fierce man, with a large moustache and high riding boots polished so much that they shone like glass. If we met him in the hall or in one of the corridors, we flattened ourselves against the wall to let him pass. But he was an honest and well-mannered man and never failed to bark a greeting as he marched by.

We soon realized that our general did not approve of what was going on. Of course, he had no time for the communist Russians. But he was also scornful of the Nazis and, particularly, of the Arrow Cross. Agi once overheard him saying that, if he had his way, they should both be made to swap their uniforms for prison clothes.

After we had been at the house a few days, some of the women went to see the general and asked if he would help make our lives a little easier. He didn't say anything at the time, but the next morning we saw him march over to the German headquarters and demand to be let in. He came out half an hour later, red-faced and sweating. There was no change in the way we were treated.

We organized all kinds of activities – keep-fit classes, concerts and plays – to keep ourselves busy. One evening, Katie and I sang a duet – *The Little Shepherd Girl* – in front of the whole house. I don't think it sounded very good, but everyone clapped and said it was marvellous. A woman in the front row wept all the way through, soaking the front of her dress. Her two sons had joined the army the day war broke out and she had not heard from them since.

The day after the concert Mother woke us early and led us into the living-room. There, pale, thin and unshaven, sat Father. With gasps of astonishment, we rushed forward and kissed him. We didn't dare make a noise in case we woke the warden, so our kisses had to speak for themselves. Mother stood to one side and watched. I glanced up to see if I could tell what she was thinking. Her handsome face was fixed, like a mask. Many years later she confessed to me, 'I didn't have one happy day with your father.'

Speaking in a whisper, Father told us his story. Life in the Workers' Brigades was unspeakable. They were given impossible jobs, such as clearing mines with their bare hands. Their officers, the worst in the army, beat them regularly. Anyone suspected of shirking was shot.

Father realized he would die if he did not get away and had managed to escape. Somehow he had made his way to Budapest and found our new house. Now he was going to join the resistance, bands of fighters that attacked the Germans behind their lines.

The next night he was gone. He had returned to fight evil his way, with heart and body. That left Mother, like a lioness with her cubs, to continue the fight her way, with heart and mind.

Nine

Mother's Little Victory

One morning, shortly after Father had left, there was shooting in the street outside. Katie and I looked at each other, then carried on with our game of cards. Living next door to the SS headquarters, we were used to such sounds. It usually meant the execution of some poor soul suspected of being anti-German.

This time, however, it was different. Katie was just dealing a new hand when we heard shouting coming from the kitchen. I got up and went to see what was going on. Quietly pushing open the door, I found Mother faced by two burly SS men. I let out a gasp of astonishment.

Hearing me, one of the soldiers swung round, drew his revolver and pointed it straight at me. I fled in terror back to our bedroom.

The SS man followed, shouting at me in German to come back. A couple of minutes later he had rounded up all five of us and herded us into the kitchen.

'Someone shot at us,' explained the first soldier in broken Hungarian. He was a spotty young man with straight, fair hair that stuck out like hay from under his metal helmet. 'The shots came from this building. Your mother was on the balcony, so she did the shooting. She is under arrest and will come with us.'

I couldn't believe what I had heard. My world was at an end. If they took away Mother, we'd die of starvation in a few days. We couldn't survive without her.

Mother's calm voice cut across the silence. 'I am very sorry that you have been shot at, sir. But it wasn't me. Yes, I was on the balcony, but I don't have a gun. So how could I have shot at you?'

'Liar!' shouted the second soldier, waving his revolver in front of her. 'Jewish cow, of course you have a gun!' He paused for a moment, as if he had just thought of something, then went on, 'Right, I will search your flat and find the weapon.' Leaving us with his colleague, he disappeared into the living-room.

After much banging and scraping, he came back empty-handed. He did not look flustered, which surprised me. Instead, he bowed neatly to Mother and said quite politely, 'Very well, I didn't find the gun. But I am warning you, you are under suspicion. We will be back.' With that, he clicked his heels and the two of them left the flat. We heard them laughing as they went down the stairs.

As soon as they had gone, Mother went into the living-room and picked up a corner of the carpet. There, black and gleaming, was a German revolver. 'Just as I thought,' she muttered. Telling us not to touch the weapon and to shut ourselves in our rooms, she put on her best dress, tidied her hair and left the flat. I couldn't resist seeing what would happen and crept over to the window to watch.

Ignoring the curfew, Mother went out of the house into the street. She took no notice of the two SS men, who were lounging against a lamppost, and turned right towards the German headquarters. Luckily, a group of regular army officers was standing by the iron gates. Picking out the most senior one, Mother went straight up to him and started speaking.

Mother's air of gracious authority touched all but the most hardened thugs. The officer called the SS men to him and ordered them to produce their revolvers. The holster of the one who had searched our flat was empty. All of them then turned and walked quickly towards our house. I darted back into the bedroom.

Mother led the search party straight to the living-room and showed them the revolver. The army officer picked it up and handed it back to the SS man. They stayed there arguing for a few minutes before clumping down the stairs and back to their own building.

Mother collapsed exhausted into a chair. We stood and stared at her in admiration.

'You're the best mother in the world!' gasped Agi.

'And the bravest,' said Katie.

'The cleverest, too,' I added. 'Those SS thugs won't be back in a hurry!'

Mother looked up wearily. 'Won't be back, Bandi? You wait! They haven't even started yet.'

Ten

Alone

In mid–October Hungary surrendered to the Russians. The Germans immediately set up a Hungarian government of their own. The Arrow Cross was delighted and, with German backing, stepped up its campaign against the Jews.

Shut in our apartment block, we had little idea what was happening. Rumours blew through the corridors like leaves on the autumn wind. We were about to be set free . . . we were going to be sent to death camps . . . the British were going to flatten the city with bombs. Everything was uncertain.

Arrowers burst in one morning in a tempest of hatred. Shouting and waving their weapons, they ordered everyone down to the inner courtyard. Katie brought her favourite china doll with her. Seeing it, one of the thugs snatched it from her hand and threw it against the wall. Like our hopes, it smashed into a hundred pieces.

When the Arrowers had checked our names, they sent the head of every family back to their flat to bring down their valuables. The Arrowers demanded everything: money, jewellery, watches and clocks, china and even expensive clothes. Mother's face showed no emotion as she handed over her beautiful Dresden vase.

Those who wouldn't co-operate were treated with terrible cruelty. One woman refused to hand over her wedding ring. The guard punched her to the ground and kicked her viciously until he was too tired to raise his boot.

After the looting, the leader of the gang went up to the balcony. 'Listen, filth!' he shouted. 'We're sending you on holiday, so do as you're told. Women and children to my left, men to my right. Move!'

I stayed with Mother and the girls. A soldier noticed this and pointed with his stick towards the line of men near the gate. 'You!' he barked. 'Get over there!' I hesitated and looked at Mother. Her lips moved slightly but no words came.

'I said, get over there, Jewish scum!' The man raised his stick to beat me.

'Excuse me, sir,' said Mother, speaking slowly and carefully, 'but my son is young. I'd be most grateful, sir, if you'd allow him to stay with us.'

The man turned and looked at her. The strange, dignified request had confused him. Perhaps for a moment he was reminded of his own childhood, his own mother?

The shouts of other soldiers broke the spell, but he did not hit me. Lowering his stick, he said automatically, as if reciting his orders, 'There are to be no exceptions. Your son will join the men. Now!'

When I had crossed the yard to the column of men, I turned and looked back towards the others. Mother was holding Katie and Edith by the hand and talking to Agi. As I gazed at them, Agi looked up and saw me. She touched Mother on the elbow and she, too, turned her head towards me. Swallowing hard, I lifted my hand and gave a little wave. Mother and Agi smiled back at me. Katie waved her handkerchief. My eyes filled with tears.

A hand grasped my wrist. It was Mr Solomon, the old man from the flat below ours. 'I know, Bandi,' he said, nodding his head slowly. 'It's terrible. But you are the future, you know. It's no good you giving up.'

As he spoke, the guards yelled at us to get moving. The iron gates of the courtyard swung open and we were herded into the street. 'Hurry up, you lazy animals!' screamed a guard in an Arrow Cross uniform several sizes too small for him. 'We haven't got all day!'

'Where are we going?' someone behind me asked.

The guard laughed. 'Where all dregs go! Down the drain! Now get a move on.' To make his point, he slammed the butt of his rifle across Mr Solomon's back. The old man bent almost double with pain. I put out my hand to help him. With his black clothes and long white beard he looked so innocent – the ideal grandfather, utterly harmless.

'Thank you, Bandi,' he croaked, pulling himself upright.

After we had gone a bit further, I looked across at him.

He was obviously in great pain and finding it difficult to walk. I wondered what I could say to encourage him. Stooping down so he could hear me, I whispered, 'Don't worry, Mr Solomon. I won't give up. I promise.'

They were brave words, but I'm not sure that I meant them. Never in my life had I felt so lonely and so afraid.

Eleven

The People's Park

It was on that morning that my numbness started. I don't mean anything physical – although I was very thin, I was still in good health. It was my heart that went numb.

No adult should witness what I witnessed that day, let alone a child. It was a world gone mad, hell rising up to take over the Earth. Knives of cruelty cut the connection between my senses and my emotions. I saw, heard and smelt, but I did not feel.

I did not choose or even want it that way. It just happened. If it had not, then I would have gone mad. All I was left with was an unbreakable determination to survive.

The long column of Jews – men, women and children – walked between lines of Arrow Cross thugs, soldiers and police across the silent city. We were beaten, kicked, spat at and scorned.

At one point we halted in a small, tree-lined square. There was fighting going on. Soldiers darted between the trees, firing up at a red-brick house on the corner. One

41

Arrower said it was a nest of 'Jewish bandits'.

I thought of Father and his resistance fighters – was he there, so near us yet so impossibly far away? Like a scene in a newsreel, a huge Tiger tank rolled up. Its gun roared and a gaping, smoking hole appeared in the front of the house. There was no more shooting.

The guards screamed at us to get moving again. Mr Solomon had sat down on the kerb, utterly exhausted. A soldier came up and kicked him in the leg. 'Get up, you old scarecrow!' he yelled.

Mr Solomon did not protest or beg for mercy. He just sat and looked at nothing with his watery blue eyes. I'm sure he had decided that this was the end.

The soldier turned to his sergeant. 'What shall I do with him, sir?'

'Shoot him!'

As the gun went off, Mr Solomon shook but did not fall over. He just collapsed inside himself, still looking nowhere.

Someone behind me muttered, 'Blessed are the dead.' It was a prayer of despair.

We were taken to the People's Park. Before the war it had been a place of fairs and circuses. I remember going there one evening with Mother and Katie to watch a troupe of clowns from Romania. Katie had laughed so much she fell off her seat and squashed the hat of the woman in front of us.

As we went through the park gates, I turned round and

looked for her. I couldn't see her, but I knew she wasn't laughing this time.

When everyone was inside the park, we were told to sit down and wait. It was now afternoon and we had had nothing to eat or drink since breakfast. It was cold, too. A chill wind blew from the east, plucking the leaves from the trees and sending them scudding and spiralling over the grey carpet of humanity laid over the damp grass.

As it was beginning to get dark, the lorries arrived. Speeding through the gates, they spread out and stopped with their tailboards facing us. A whistle blew and with one movement the backs of the lorries opened. From each one projected the muzzle of a machine gun.

'This is it,' said the man sitting next to me. He was wearing a shiny bowler hat, his little gesture of dignity. I remember wondering how he had managed to keep it on after all we had been through.

'Are they going to shoot us?' I asked. My voice sounded unreal, as if it came from someone else.

'No point in all those guns otherwise,' said the man. 'They're just waiting for the signal.'

The signal didn't come. I'll never know why. Perhaps the orders had been misunderstood? Or maybe they couldn't think what to do with the bodies afterwards? Anyway, after a couple of hours the machine guns were suddenly withdrawn and the lorries drove off into the darkness. Without food or shelter, we were left in the park all night. It was freezing cold – too cold for many of the elderly, sick and injured.

At dawn we were told we could go home. Stiff and starving, I got to my feet and went to look for Mother and the girls. When we found each other, we hardly said a word. We just stared at each other, kissed and began the weary tramp back to the Star House.

We were among the last to leave the park. At the gates, I stopped and looked back. The grass was strewn with the bodies of those who had died in the night.

Twelve

The Safe Pass

Back in our Star House, we lived like hunted animals. Any day, any moment, the Germans or the Arrow Cross might round us up and send us to our deaths. Sooner or later our turn was bound to come.

It was around this time that we heard of safe passes. These were special documents, issued by a neutral country, that put an individual under that country's protection. In theory, the Germans could not then touch them.

Mother learned that a Swedish diplomat, Raoul Wallenberg, was handing out safe passes from his office. Every day she tried to get there. Sometimes the warden of our house would not allow her out. When she did manage to reach Wallenberg's office, the crowd outside was so great she returned empty-handed.

Just when it looked as if we'd never get a pass, a stranger came to the house. He said he was working for the Pope and could get safe passes for everyone who wanted them.

Mother was immediately suspicious. 'What's the catch?' she asked.

The man smiled at her. 'There's no catch, madam. I have the Pope's authority to give a free pass to every Christian.'

That, of course, was the catch. To get a pass, Jews had to be baptized into the Christian faith. Mother would have nothing to do with the scheme, but she was fair minded and asked us what we thought. While sharing her religious views, I was prepared to go through a Christian ceremony if it would save us. We would still be Jews, after all, I told myself, and I was sure that God would understand. I accepted the stranger's proposal.

A few days later, a Roman Catholic priest turned up. He was a plump, pink man who smelt of soap and cigars. He checked my name, spoke for a few minutes about starting a new life, then sprinkled water from a glass bottle on my head. He then muttered some words in a strange language (I know now that it was Latin) and gave me a wafer to eat. I knew the taste: earlier in the war I had eaten wafers that my Christian friends had stolen from their church.

When the ceremony was over, the priest blessed me and announced proudly, 'You are a Christian now, Andrew.' He insisted on calling me Andrew rather than my proper name, Andor. From his briefcase he drew out an important-looking document with our family name on it. 'Jesus Christ has saved you all, Andrew,' he said, handing it to me. I thanked him and put the document in a safe place. I felt only a little guilty at what I had done.

★ ★ ★

Two days later we were moved to a different Star House. This time we had no cart for our belongings and had to carry everything by hand. The new apartment block was less smart than the last one, but at least we had a small flat to ourselves. It had two main rooms, a kitchen and a toilet. As before, Mother soon had it feeling like home.

There was also a locked door in the flat. As I was always on the lookout for hiding places, I asked the warden, a tall man with a face like an ostrich, what was in there. 'Mind your own business!' he snapped. 'It's a box room of private possessions, so don't you go near it.'

Winter was now closing in and we were desperate for money to buy food and fuel. Mother did washing and other odd jobs for Jews who had somehow managed to keep their money. The work was very tiring and left her hands red and rough. But I never once heard her complain.

I was able to help, too. Out shopping, Agi met an old friend who ran a paper factory. When he heard our story, he took pity on us and asked Agi if I would like a job. I was extremely grateful for his kindness: if the authorities had found him employing a Jew, he would almost certainly have been shot.

Every morning for the next four weeks I put on a plain coat, sneaked out of the house and made my way to the factory. My work involved rolling huge bundles of paper from the storeroom to a cutting machine. The factory owner paid me each evening. 'It's better like that, Bandi,' he explained. 'After all, who knows where you might be tomorrow?'

Thirteen

The Visitor

As I was stealing through the back streets on my way to work at the factory, I sometimes saw Jews being rounded up in dawn raids. The operation was planned by the SS, who stood and watched as the Arrowers carried out the dirty work. They usually cleared two or three Star Houses at a time. The Jewish residents were forced into the road, beaten and searched, then marched away to begin their final journey.

I soon worked out that the Nazis were working to a pattern, moving through the city district by district. Each raid brought them closer to where we lived. I explained to the others what was going on.

'We could sit tight and hope the Russians reach the city before the Nazis reach us,' suggested Agi.

Edith shuddered. 'And if the Russians don't get through? They aren't exactly going to speed up their advance just to save the Guttmann family.'

'Yes, I agree, Edith,' I said. 'I vote we try to get out. We've still got the safe pass the priest gave us, haven't we?'

After a bit more discussion, we decided to make a move as soon as possible. Mother outlined her emergency plan in case we were split up: we should adopt the Hungarian family name 'Boross' and try to meet at an apartment block in the centre of the city. Mother had heard that the landlady, Miss Kádár, always had rooms to rent.

The next morning we packed our things in suitcases, cut the Stars of David off our coats and, around midday, walked boldly out of the house. It was curfew time, when Jews found on the streets could be shot on sight.

As usual, there was a pair of Arrow Cross guards lounging on the pavement opposite. As soon as they saw us, they told us to halt. My heart was pounding.

'Come here, scum!' one of them ordered.

Trying to look as casual as possible, we crossed to their side of the road.

'What are you doing out?' the man asked.

Mother smiled at him. 'Good afternoon, officer,' she began. 'I think you will find we have the necessary papers.' She took out the priest's pass and handed it to the guard. We held our breath and waited.

The guard read the paper very slowly, mouthing the words with his lips. I wondered whether he actually understood what he was reading. When he had finished, he folded the pass neatly and held it out towards Mother. I thought he was going to give it back. Instead, very slowly, he tore it into tiny pieces.

'Nice try, Jew,' he laughed, dropping the remains of our

pass into the gutter. 'Now you and your stinking family get back in the house before someone shoots you.' He began to take his rifle off his shoulder.

Without a word, we turned and walked back across the street. I half expected him to shoot us in the back, but nothing happened. Five minutes later we were in our flat. As Mother and Agi began sewing on the Stars of David again, Katie crept into the corner and wept.

I don't know how Father found us. Maybe he had secretly contacted my employer at the paper factory. I don't know how he got into the house without being seen, either. But he managed it somehow and, just like the last visit, when we woke up in the morning, there he was.

But this time it was different. As we rushed forward to greet him, he raised his hand. 'No, please, be careful!' he whispered. 'I'm not in very good shape.' Only then did we notice his wound.

He had been shot in the left leg. The place where the bullet had hit him was wrapped in a dirty bandage, but the rest of the leg was black and blue. Although he needed urgent medical attention, this was impossible. If we called a doctor or took him to hospital, they would immediately want to know how he had been injured. All we could do was clean his wound and try to make him comfortable. Everything had to be done in silence. The warden, Ostrich-face, was always snooping about, trying to listen in on other people's conversations.

* * *

The raid came three days after Father's arrival. We were woken by the sound of boots running up the stairs. There was a loud hammering at our door.

'Jews out!' shouted a voice. 'Any trouble and you'll all be shot! Get a move on!'

My heart sank. This, surely, was the beginning of the end.

Fourteen

The Key

The raiders were going from door to door, making sure everyone was awake. While they were banging on the door of the neighbouring flat, we helped Father hide under a bed then returned to the living-room. Just as we did so, the soldiers burst in.

There were four Arrowers and an SS officer carrying a clipboard. 'Right,' said the officer with a yawn, 'what pigs have we in this sty?'

'A woman and four kids,' answered one of the Arrowers.

The officer glanced at his list. 'Yes. Guttmann.' He ran his eyes quickly over us. 'Mmm, we'll take that one.' He pointed his pencil at Agi. 'We can always find work for a pretty girl, can't we?' The other Arrowers sniggered. One of them stepped forward and grabbed Agi by the arm. She shuddered and tried to move away from him.

'Now then, darling,' he sneered, 'don't let's have any trouble! Get outside!' He pushed her across the room towards the door.

Mother's lips were trembling and tears filled her eyes. She

took half a step towards the officer and pleaded, 'Please, sir, she's only young. Take me instead.'

'You?' he laughed. 'You must be joking!'

Another of the Arrowers waved his gun in my direction. 'What about that one?'

The officer shook his head. 'Not now. I've got enough for the moment. We'll come back for the rest tomorrow.' With that they turned and left the flat, pushing Agi in front of them. She was wearing only her thin indoor dress and the party shoes Mother had given her for her sixteenth birthday.

We stood in shocked silence for several minutes. Eventually, Mother walked across the room and shut the front door. Her face was a sheet of crumpled paper. 'We must pray for Agi, children,' she said quietly. 'Only God can help her now.'

During the two hours Jews were allowed out to go shopping, Mother and I returned to Raoul Wallenberg's office. Once again there was a huge crowd outside jostling to get in.

'Not a hope,' said Mother with a sigh. 'We'll have to try to get here early tomorrow morning.'

'But that's when the Arrowers are coming back,' I said.

She nodded. 'I know, Bandi. We'll just have to find a way of avoiding them.'

That evening we discussed what we could do. The building was surrounded by guards, so escape was impossible. Our only hope was to hide. But where? I mentioned the box room and suggested breaking the lock.

'Pointless,' said Edith. 'When they see the smashed lock, they'll know where we are at once.'

'Couldn't we unlock it?' suggested Katie.

'Oh, yes?' I laughed. 'Shall I go and ask Ostrich-face for his key?'

Katie looked at me crossly. 'Don't be silly, Bandi. Listen, there are lots of empty flats now and they've all still got the keys in their locks. I bet one of them will fit.'

Mother nodded. 'It's worth a try, Katie. It's about our only hope.'

Later that night, when the warden had gone to bed, Edith and I slipped out and collected a dozen keys from flats nearby. After trying several of them, we found one that fitted. The door creaked open. Mother lit a match and by its light we saw that the room was piled high with furniture, carpets and other household objects.

'Perfect!' she whispered. 'Now put back the keys we don't need and try to get some sleep.'

Just before dawn Mother unlocked the door again and we clambered over the furniture to the back of the room. We had great difficulty getting Father in, but somehow we managed it and settled him down on a rug with a cardboard box as a pillow. I looked at him anxiously. He was in great pain and running a fever. I knew he couldn't last much longer without proper medical help.

In our hurry to get into the room I had forgotten to go to

the toilet. After we had lain there for about an hour, I was bursting. When I told Father, he whispered, 'Not here, Bandi. Hold it in!'

'I can't!' I hissed.

'You must!'

Mother's voice came through the darkness. 'Let him, if he has to.'

Father did not reply and I relieved myself beside the wall where I was lying.

Shortly afterwards we heard the raiders marching up the stairs.

Fifteen

Farewell

The SS officer and Arrowers had come to clear the house. As on the previous day, they hammered on the doors, then burst in and drove their victims out into the street. Lying in our hiding place, we listened anxiously as the shouts and curses of the soldiers mingled with the pleas of the mothers and the pitiful crying of the children.

Gradually, over the noise, I became aware of another sound: the snuffling and scratching of dogs. I was seized with panic. If they entered our room the dogs would be bound to sniff us out, especially after what I had done. We'd be captured – maybe shot straight away – and it would be my fault. Tormented by the sharp smell of urine in my nostrils, I started to shake. My mother stirred. I thought she was going to tell me to lie still. Instead, she stretched out her hand and began very gently to stroke the back of my head. A lifetime of self-sacrifice was in that simple, loving gesture. My heart beat more slowly and I lay still.

'What's in here?' asked a voice beyond the door.

'Just old furniture. Most of it belongs to Colonel Weber. They can't hide there. The door's always locked and I've got the only key.' It was Ostrich-face. He sounded annoyed.

The officer was not impressed. 'Oh, yes? Well, go and get the key and open it up. Now!'

While Ostrich-face went to fetch the key, I heard a dog scratching at the door with its paw.

The key scraped in the lock. I froze as light flooded into the room from the open door. 'See, it's full of Jews!' said the warden sarcastically. 'Jewish chairs, Jewish carpets—'

'Shut up!' barked the officer. Someone began to move the furniture nearest the door. A dog whined.

'Listen, officer, it's only furniture. The family must have escaped during the night.'

'All right, all right!' The German had had enough. 'But someone's going to answer for this. Lock it up again and let's get going.'

The door closed, the key turned and we were left alone in the dark.

We waited for about fifteen minutes, then unlocked the door and crept out into our flat. Everyone had gone. The house was eerily still and silent, as if no one had lived there for years. Moving as quietly as possible, we made our way on to the landing, down the stairs and into the hall. Father led the way, leaning heavily on a stick.

The warden's flat was on the right, near the front door. As we were passing it, he suddenly emerged. I don't know who was more surprised, he or us. A look of terror came into his eyes as it dawned on him that we must have been in the locked room all along. If the SS discovered what he'd done, he was finished.

Quivering with fury, he screamed, 'Filthy, tricking swine! Don't move! Wait here!' Before we could stop him, he darted out of the front door and locked it behind him.

'Oh, God of Abraham protect us!' muttered Father. 'We must get out before he comes back with the soldiers.' Leaving him there, the rest of us rushed into the ground-floor rooms to check the windows. They were all heavily barred and the back door was also locked. We were trapped.

Katie's shout of glee brought us running back into the hall. She was brandishing a large key with a label on it. 'Spare front door key!' she read. 'It was on the rack in the warden's flat. Come on!'

Seconds later, we were hurrying into the street. A thin, cold rain was falling and there was not a soul to be seen.

Expecting to be stopped at any moment, we made our way to a main shopping street and lost ourselves in the crowd. Outside a baker's shop we paused to get our breath back.

Father was sweating and very pale. 'Listen,' he panted, 'you can't wait for me. I must get to the hospital. So, for the moment, goodbye.'

One by one we held him in our arms and kissed him. I felt drained of emotion as my lips brushed his hot, stubbled cheek. Then we stood, huddled together against the rain, and watched as he limped slowly away. We all knew we would never see him again.

Sixteen

The Swedish Flag

My mind was blank as we trudged through the wet streets towards Raoul Wallenberg's office. I didn't want to think. Agi had gone, Father had gone, we had nowhere to live, no money and we could be arrested at any moment. It was best to remain numb, not daring to think or even hope.

But hope would not die. It had stopped raining when we reached the square where Wallenberg's office stood. The crowds that had milled about the building on our last visit had gone. As I looked up at the yellow-and-blue Swedish flag flying from the roof, the sky behind it suddenly brightened. The white clouds parted and a thin ray of winter sunshine lit up the square. It was a sign, I told myself. A sign of hope.

We kept out of sight while Mother went to see if she could get a pass. She was, she told us when she came out, one of the last Jews to be granted a Swedish safe pass. All the other Jews in the city had either got one or been taken away. Armed with the pass, we set out for a house the Swedes had set aside for Jewish refugees. It was easy enough to find. But outside stood an Arrow Cross patrol, snarling like guard dogs at anyone who came near.

We hesitated, remembering what had happened to the pass we got from the priest, then walked boldly up to the door. To our surprise, the guards gave us no trouble. They glanced at our pass, laughed, and let us straight in. When we got inside, we saw immediately what had amused them. The place was teeming with refugees. At least a hundred people were packed into each room. Others stood in rows along corridors. The floorboards groaned dangerously with the weight of people. The blocked toilets overflowed on to the floor. The stench and noise were unbearable. This was no place to stay.

After a quick look around, Mother led us back outside.

The guards found our exit even more amusing. 'Moving on?' one of them mocked. 'Most pigs like a good sty. Not dirty enough for you, eh?'

The man next to him roared with laughter. 'Buzz off then,' he smirked. 'But you won't get far. I might even shoot you as you're walking across the square – bit of target practice.'

Mother shepherded us past them without a word. When we were out of earshot, she whispered, 'Don't worry! They won't dare shoot so near the Swedish house.'

She was right. We crossed the square safely and set out for the house of a non-Jewish friend in the suburbs of Buda.

I'll never know why we were not stopped. Although not

wearing Stars of David, it must have been obvious that a mother and her thin, bedraggled children were Jews on the run. But no one challenged us. Perhaps they didn't care any more? When we halted for a rest, we could hear Russian guns in the distance. I never thought I would find the sound of gunfire encouraging. But I did then. With each dull boom I imagined the Russians advancing under their red star banners to our rescue.

Occasionally we passed small groups of Jews being marched into the countryside. The sight should have horrified me. Instead, I stared at them blankly, refusing to take in what I saw. What could I do, anyway? War had made Budapest into a jungle where it was each person for themselves.

We walked for most of the day, over the river by one of the few bridges still standing, past bombed shops and offices and out into the green suburbs. The houses here were larger and stood amid neat gardens behind high walls and iron gates. Eventually Mother found the address she was looking for and rang the brass hand bell.

An elderly woman in a blue-and-white dress came to the gate. The moment she saw us a look of terror came into her face. Hurrying us into the house, she looked around anxiously as she shut the front door.

'Oh, dear!' she began. 'What a state you're in! I mean, I do want to help you, Mrs Guttmann. Of course I do. But – I'm sure you understand – if anyone finds out . . .' Her voice trailed into silence.

The Nazis killed charity long before they started killing Jews. We were going to have to move on.

Seventeen

The Drain

The woman let us stay overnight as long as we promised to leave at dawn. We held a family conference. Our best chance was to split up, Mother said. She and Katie, pretending to be refugees fleeing the Russians, would return to the city to find work and rent one of the flats in Miss Kádár's apartment block. Edith and I would move to a house Wallenberg had set up for Jewish children, managed by the Swiss Red Cross. Mother reckoned we'd be safe there until the war was over.

The next morning Mother escorted Edith and me to the Red Cross house. After reminding us of Miss Kádár's address, she and Katie left. The parting reminded me of a previous farewell – a few hugs and kisses but no tears or sad words. The numbness had spread to everyone by now.

The Red Cross house was a dull, two-storey building that had been used by the Germans before Wallenberg bought it. It was crowded, but not as bad as the Swedish house had been. I nodded to the other boys and girls and told them my name if they asked. At night I talked a little to the boys on either side of me in the dormitory, but I did not have the heart to make friends.

As was my custom, before I settled down in the Red Cross house I explored it thoroughly for hiding places, entrances and exits. Going down to the cellar to check it out as an air-raid shelter, I found a dozen adults living there.

At the back, low down in one of the walls, I came across a large hole. I poked my head in and discovered it was an old drain that seemed to lead to a manhole on a piece of waste ground at the back of the house.

I can't remember how long Edith and I stayed in the Red Cross house. A week, maybe? But I do remember leaving it.

We were woken one morning by shouting from the street at the front of the house. I went to the window and looked out. An Arrow Cross gang was standing at the gate, demanding to be let in. One of them was beating at the lock with a sledge hammer. Without waiting to see any more, I ran to find Edith.

She must have known that I was coming because she was standing outside the girls' dormitory, wearing her coat and clutching her spare pair of shoes. 'Quick!' I whispered. 'Follow me!'

We raced down to the cellar. I expected to find the place in chaos. Instead, everyone was standing like dummies, paralysed with fear. Their eyes hardly flickered as we dashed past them towards the drain.

'Urgh!' exclaimed Edith when she saw it. 'I can't go down there, Bandi!'

'No choice,' I muttered. I shoved my head and shoulders into the hole and began scrambling away from the house on all fours. After I had gone about ten metres, I stopped and listened. Thank goodness! Edith was following along behind me.

Reaching the end of the tunnel, I pushed up the manhole cover and looked about. It was a misty morning and there was no one in sight. Five minutes later Edith and I were hurrying down the main road in what we hoped was the direction of the city.

After we had walked for about an hour, the mist cleared and I noticed the houses were fewer and further apart. We passed the occasional farm, too. Edith noticed the same thing. 'Bandi,' she suggested, 'do you think we're going the wrong way? I mean, further from the city.'

I stopped. 'Yes, I reckon you're right, Edith. Come on! Back we go!'

'Lucky I brought my spare shoes,' she said as we turned and started to retrace out steps. 'My others will be worn out by the time we get there.'

Although it wasn't very funny, we both roared with laughter. Neither of us had laughed like that for ages. It must have been the relief. A little later we looked up at the white clouds scudding across the pale winter sky. Edith thought they made our world seem small and unimportant. 'I bet there's another one out there,' she said.

'Another what?'

'Another world. Like ours, except fairer.'

'Maybe,' I muttered. 'But it's a heck of a long way away.'

When the Red Cross house came in sight, we slowed down and approached with caution. There was no need. It was empty and abandoned. The only sign that children had once lived there was a small teddy bear lying in the road outside.

We passed by without a word and continued on our way to the city.

Eighteen

Miss Kádár

Edith and I reached the address Mother had given us in the middle of the afternoon. It was a grand, five-storey building at the heart of the city. For some reason it had a green dome on top, like an observatory. We were much more interested in the cinema in the basement. As Mother had told us not to contact her before dark, we spent some time reading the cinema posters and trying to imagine what the movies were like.

When we got bored with this, we crossed the road to try and guess which was Mother's flat. As I turned, I noticed a familiar figure in a tweed suit walking briskly towards me. It was Dr Nagy, the man who had taught me Hungarian at secondary school.

The hairs rose up on the back of my neck. Nagy was a fair man but rather strict. Far worse, he was fiercely pro-German. To my horror, I realized he was looking straight at me. There was no time to hide, so I did the only thing I could: I stared straight back at him. Our eyes met. It was like a battle of wills, each daring the other to look away first.

Neither of us blinked. He walked right up to me, still staring, then passed by and continued on his way.

I like to think that Nagy spared me because I stood up to him or because he liked me. But it may have been because he knew the German cause was lost. The Russians were only a few kilometres from Budapest now and the sound of gunfire echoed over the city most of the time.

Mother came back from work just as it was getting dark. Standing in the porch of the apartment block, we spotted her and started waving before she saw us. When she realized who we were, for a fraction of a second her face lit up in a smile. Then, just as swiftly, it creased into a frown. By the time she reached us, her lips were smiling again. But not her eyes.

'My darling, Joseph!' she cried, hugging me so tight I could hardly breathe, let alone speak. 'And you, Elizabeth,' she went on, smothering Edith as well. 'How lucky the Boross family is! How did you escape the Russians? Are you hurt? Come, tell me all!'

I thought she had gone mad. What terrible thing had happened to make her forget the names of her own children? And she seemed afflicted with a dreadful twitch that made her blink all the time.

Gradually releasing us from her grip, she continued to bombard us with questions. 'How is the farm, Joseph? Who's looking after the cows, Elizabeth? Joseph, are you sure the Russians didn't hurt you? Oh, this is the greatest day the Boross family has ever seen!'

I was finding it hard not to cry. All Mother's efforts had come to this! Madness! I glanced up into her face. She was looking hard at me and still blinking. Or was it winking?

Then I realized what was happening. Of course! She had not just changed her name to 'Mrs Boross' – that wouldn't have deceived anyone for long. She had also invented Christian first names for her children and a whole new familyhistory! I glanced over at Edith and saw that she, too, understood.

'Elizabeth,' I said slowly, 'let's go inside with Mother and tell her our story.'

'Of course, Joseph,' she grinned.

As we turned to enter the apartment block, we saw why Mother had needed to act so swiftly. A tall, elegant woman in a fur coat was standing on the doorstep. 'Good evening, Mrs Boross,' she said kindly. 'What a happy occasion!'

'Happier than I can say, Miss Kádár,' smiled Mother. 'My missing children, Joseph and Elizabeth, whom I thought were dead, have escaped the Russians and found their way here. It is a miracle!'

She took me by the hand and urged me forward. 'Miss Kádár,' she said politely, 'may I introduce my son Joseph and my daughter Elizabeth?' Edith and I bowed. 'Miss Kádár is my landlady,' explained Mother, 'one of the kindest in all Budapest. A clever lady, too,' she added. 'There is very little she does not understand.'

After a few more words, Miss Kádár went out into the street and we escaped to Mother's flat.

Nineteen

The Piano

We soon told each other our stories. Mother was horrified but not surprised to hear of the Arrow Cross attack on a Red Cross house. 'Now they know Germany's going to be defeated,' she said, 'they're worse than ever. Got nothing to lose, I suppose. Please, *please* be careful! Especially of Miss Kádár.'

Our landlady was passionately pro-Nazi. She believed the Russian communists were the real enemy, and every day she expected to hear that the British and Americans had joined the Germans against the 'Red Devils'. What then for the Jews? I thought. I hoped Miss Kádár's dream was as unrealistic as it sounded.

Mother had somehow got hold of forged papers. As 'Mrs Boross' she had found work as a cleaner and cook in a large boarding house. The job was ideal because she could steal food and smuggle it home for us. Without it I think we would have starved to death.

Edith, Katie and I were trapped in the flat. Outside, papers were checked all the time. The false ones Mother had got us were not very realistic. We couldn't wander around the building, either, in case we ran into Miss Kádár. Although she didn't suspect us, she might ask about our background and realize our story was not the same as Mother's. It was almost worse than being in a Star House. There everyone knew who we were. Now we were living a dangerous lie.

I left the flat only once, after seeing Miss Kádár go out. Wandering downstairs, I found a piano in the hall. Gingerly, never having played before, I struck a few notes. What magic! The simple sound lifted my soul. I tried to pick out a tune and was so enthralled that I didn't notice a fat man emerge from a nearby flat and stand listening. When I paused, we exchanged a few words. Without saying it, we each knew the other was a Jew.

One evening just before Christmas, as we were getting ready for bed, there was a sharp knock at the door. Mother opened it and stepped back in dismay. On the mat were two young SS officers. Between them, smiling brightly, stood Agi.

To our amazement, the officers were models of politeness and good manners. 'We are delighted to return your charming daughter, Mrs Boross,' explained one of them. 'You will find she is well and unharmed.' Mother thanked them. Promising to visit Agi again, they clicked their heels, saluted and left the flat.

Mother exploded with anger. How could Agi stoop so

low? Going out with Nazis – the brutes trying to exterminate her own people! Agi waited patiently until Mother
had calmed down, then told us her remarkable story.

After being taken from the Star House, she had joined a
large column of Jews forced to walk hundreds of kilometres
to Austria. Two weeks later, she and a friend collapsed by
the roadside.

When their guard went off to get permission to shoot
them, the girls had an amazing piece of good luck. A passing
Hungarian farmer took pity on them and helped them on to
his horse-drawn cart. He drove them to the nearest railway
station, where he gave them money for tickets to Budapest.

The train was packed with drunken German soldiers who
gave the two pretty girls a rough time. Goodness knows
what would have happened if the two SS officers had not
intervened, rescuing Agi and her friend and escorting them
back to their families in Budapest. Fortunately, Agi had
remembered the name 'Boross' and the address of Miss
Kádár's apartments.

So there we were, Mother and her children united again.
Surely, we thought, it is only a matter of days now? Somehow, anyhow, we had to stay alive until the Russians broke
through. The tension was almost unbearable. Shut up in the
flat, watching the Arrow Cross patrols in the street below,
we became tetchy and argumentative. At one point Edith
and Agi almost came to blows over whose turn it was to use
the washbasin.

★　★　★

Looking back, I realize it was bound to happen. A week after Christmas, an Arrow Cross patrol came to check Miss Kádár's apartments: the same hammering on doors, foul language and bullying. Three men entered our flat and demanded to see our papers. Mother calmly handed them over.

'Eh? What's this?' growled the leader, a huge man with angry boils on his neck. He pointed at the forged official stamp. 'Where'd you get this from, woman?'

'The same place as everyone else,' lied Mother. 'The government offices in Kossuth Street.'

The man's eyes narrowed. 'Oh, yeah? Well let's go down there and ask them, shall we? All of you out – now!'

Twenty

The Air of Freedom

'Excuse me,' said a polite voice from the corridor outside, 'but what's going on here?' It was one of the two gallant SS officers who had rescued Agi. As promised, they had both come back to visit her. Their timing was perfect. Mother stepped forward and welcomed them like old friends.

After returning her greeting, one of them asked, 'But what are these thugs doing here, Mrs Boross?' He looked angrily at the boil-necked bully.

When Mother told him the Arrowers were hassling us about our papers, he turned on them and ordered them out of the house. The officers then asked Agi if she'd like to go out with them. They looked very disappointed when she explained she had a headache and ought to stay indoors. They remained polite, however, and said they would come back when she felt better.

If they did return, they would have found the house in ruins. That night it received a direct hit from a Russian bomb. It blew a huge hole in our living-room floor but, by some miracle, left the bedrooms on either side untouched.

We now had no choice but to move down to the basement where everyone else had already taken shelter.

The basement, which had once housed the cinema, was like a medieval picture of hell. Oil-lamps flickered on the walls. A ghostly audience of corpses sat stiff and upright in the seats. Part of the floor had been cleared for use as a hospital. Exhausted doctors struggled without medicine to comfort those injured in the roaring nightmare overhead. Through the door came a constant stream of the seriously wounded – Hungarian soldiers and citizens, Germans and Arrowers carrying sacks of loot. When they died, the doctors took the sacks and shared out the contents amongst themselves. Mother and Agi worked as nurses, saving their food rations to share with the rest of us.

The Russians were in the city now, fighting their way from street to street towards the centre. Above us, the firing continued day and night. When a shell landed nearby, our building quivered and shook like a liner in a storm. The cries of fear and despair, the dust and the lingering smell of death still haunt me in my dreams.

Incredibly, in all this mayhem, the Arrow Cross went on with its grizzly work. Three times Arrowers came into the basement, shouting and demanding to see everyone's papers. Somehow Mother managed to persuade them to leave us alone. But the fat man who had listened to me playing the piano was not so fortunate. They arrested him on their last visit and marched him outside to his death in the winter darkness.

On entering the basement, I had hidden myself away in a small space between a wall and a large iron pipe. I remained there for three weeks, coming out only to go to the toilet or get food. Through the pipe, which went up to the street outside, I listened to the noises of battle – the firing, the rumble of tanks and, occasionally, the desperate cries of soldiers. Each day the firing got nearer and nearer.

One morning I was woken by a new sound. Someone was banging at the other side of the wall, trying to break through. A small hole appeared. More bricks were pushed aside and a soldier peered through the opening. A few seconds later, he squeezed into the basement, jumped to his feet and started calling out to us in a language I didn't understand. I looked at his uniform. On each shoulder was a small red star.

The Russians had arrived.

We stayed in the basement for another week. Finally, when a Russian officer told us it was safe to leave, Katie, Edith, Agi and I dragged ourselves up the stairs and out into the pale light of a January afternoon. For a few minutes we just stood there, breathing in the fresh air of freedom. Then I walked away a few steps on my own and looked around me. The city I had known so well had disappeared. In its place stretched a silent, smoking wasteland of broken buildings and rubble.

When I heard someone approaching behind me, I knew without looking who it was. 'We have survived, Bandi, darling,' Mother said quietly.

I nodded but still did not look at her. She took my hand and squeezed it. Despite the coldness of the winter air, a surge of warmth ran through me. The numbness that had held my heart for so long began to melt away, and I wept like a little child.

Historical Notes

The Nazis planned to wipe out the Jewish population in all the territories they controlled. This dreadful slaughter is known as the Holocaust. Systematic mass killings began when the Nazis introduced the Final Solution in 1942. By the end of the war, the SS was more than halfway towards its 'target figure' of exterminating 11 million Jews.

Some 825,000 Jews lived in pre-war Hungary. About two-thirds of them – 550,000 men, women and children – died in the Holocaust. At one point they were being taken off by train to SS death camps at the rate of 4,000 a day. Auschwitz in Poland was the most infamous death camp. Perhaps as many as 4 million Jews died there, many killed with poisonous gas.

On 4 July 1944 the Hungarian government realized the Nazis were probably going to lose the war and banned the further transportation of Jews to the death camps. The persecution continued, however, largely at the hands of the brutal Arrow Cross fascists. Thousands of Jews were tortured, shot or marched to Austria to work for the Nazis as slave labour. It was from one of these slave labour columns that Agi and her friend escaped.

The Russians remained in control of Hungary after the war and turned it into a communist state. The courts found hundreds of ex-Arrow Cross members guilty of murder and executed them. A bloody Hungarian uprising against the Russians failed in 1956. The communist government finally collapsed thirty-four years later and Hungary became a democracy.

The Russians captured Raoul Wallenberg after the war and imprisoned him in the Soviet Union. He was never seen again.

Andor (Bandi) Guttmann returned to his Jewish faith, which he had never abandoned in his heart, as soon as the war ended. Now living in north London, in 1994 he wrote down his memories of what he had been through. His memoires inspired the writing of this story.

Further Information

If you would like to find out more about the Holocaust in Hungary and elsewhere, these books will help:

Adams, Simon, *World War Two: Holocaust* (Franklin Watts, 2015)

Sheehan, Sean, *Moments in History: Why did the Holocaust happen?* (Wayland, 2015)

Thomson, Ruth, *Terezin – A Story of the Holocaust* (Franklin Watts, 2013)

Tong, Neil, *Documenting WWII: The Holocaust* (Wayland, 2012)

Woolf, Alex, *Children of the Holocaust* (Franklin Watts, 2014)

You can also find further information on the Internet:
Try the Simon Wiesenthal Center on:
motlc.wiesenthal.com/site

Glossary

Achtung! Warning! or Look out! (German).

Allies Britain, the US, the USSR, France and the other countries that fought together against Germany and Japan.

Arrow Cross The Hungarian fascist party led by Ferenc Szalasi. It ruled Hungary from October 1944 to January 1945, when it organized the deaths of thousands of Jews.

Artillery Heavy guns.

Barracks Accommodation for members of the armed services.

Communism A system of government first set up in Russia in 1917. The government owned all property and tightly controlled people's lives. After spreading to China, Eastern Europe and several other countries after the Second World War, communism collapsed (1989–91). Today only a few countries still have communist governments.

Curfew A ban on people leaving their houses.

Death Camps Camps set up by the Nazis for killing Jews and other 'unwanted' peoples, such as gypsies and homosexuals.

84

Democracy A system of government in which power rests with the people and their representatives. US President Abraham Lincoln said it was 'government of the people, by the people, and for the people.'

Fascism An anti-communist system of government that put all power in the hands of a dictator. It glorified war and mindless love of one's country. The first fascist government was set up by Mussolini in Italy in 1922. Hitler, the best-known fascist leader, came to power in Germany in 1933.

The Final Solution The policy, followed by the Nazis from 1942–45, to exterminate all Jews living in territories they controlled.

Forge To make a false document, such as a passport, that looks like a real one.

Holocaust The Nazis' attempt to exterminate all European Jews.

Military service Time spent in one of the armed services.

Nazi Hitler's fascist political party. 'Nazi' was short for 'National Socialist'.

Patriotic Passionately attached to one's native land.

Propaganda Political information that gives only one point of view. It tries to alter people's opinions.

Reds A slang name for Russian communists.

Refugees Those driven from their homes or countries by war, oppression, famine or natural disaster.

Resistance The movement of armed opposition to the Nazis within the countries they had occupied.

Shell An exploding bullet, usually large and fired by artillery.

Socialist The political system that says the government should ensure wealth and services are distributed fairly among all people. It is sometimes seen as a more moderate, democratic form of communism.

Soviet Union Russia's communist empire, 1922–91. It was also known as the USSR. Its emblem was the red star.

Star of David The six-pointed emblem, made up of two triangles, of the Jewish people. David was an ancient king of Israel.

Other titles in the Survivors series:

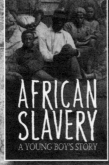

9780750296359

9780750296366

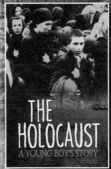

9780750296427

9780750296434

9780750296298

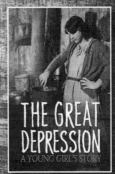

9780750296304